There is no one method or technique that is the ONLY way to learn to read. Children learn in a variety of ways. **Read with me** is an enjoyable and uncomplicated scheme that will give your child reading confidence. Through exciting stories about Kate, Tom and Sam the dog, **Read with me**:

- *teaches the first 300 key words (75% of our everyday language) plus 500 additional words*

- *stimulates a child's language and imagination through humorous, full colour illustration*

- *introduces situations and events children can relate to*

- *encourages and develops conversation and observational skills*

- *support material includes Practice and Play Books, Flash Cards, Book and Cassette Packs*

Always praise and encourage as you go along. Keep your reading sessions short.

Published by Ladybird Books Ltd
80 Strand London WC2R 0RL
A Penguin Company
11 13 15 17 19 20 18 16 14 12

Printed in Italy

Read with me
The
fierce giant

by WILLIAM MURRAY
stories by JILL CORBY
illustrated by CHRIS RUSSELL

Mother and Father are very busy. Father cuts the paper and puts it up, and Mother paints the door.

They have a lot of work to do.

Tom and Kate want to help them. But Father says, "No, Tom and Kate, you can't help us now. We are very busy here. You could take a big bit of paper and make a big picture."

He cuts off a big bit of paper and gives it to them. "You could do it in there," he tells them.

4

Tom and Kate like to make pictures,
so they take the paper. They get
everything ready to make the big
picture.

Then Tom looks at Kate.

"What picture shall we draw?" he
asks.

"Let's think," Kate tells him. "If we
think first, the picture will be a good
one."

"I know," Tom tells Kate. "We'll have a hill, a green hill."

He draws the green hill on the paper. They make it a very high green hill.

"Now," says Kate, "we'll have a castle up here. A black castle on the green hill."

They draw the black castle. It is a very high black castle.

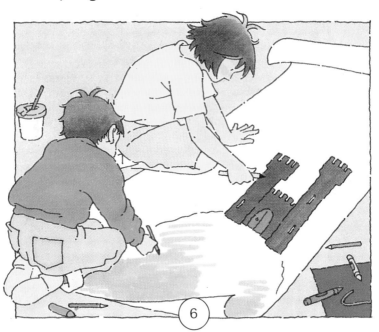

It takes them a long time. They are just as busy as their mum and dad.

''I'll draw some of these birds. Black ones going round and round high over the castle,'' Tom says.

''And I'll draw a cat, a black cat with some little ones. I'll put them up here by the castle,'' Kate tells him.

''How about a big giant?'' asks Tom. ''We'll put him here by his castle.''

''Yes,'' says Kate. ''The castle could be the giant's home.''

"We could cut these bits out to make the giant," Kate tells Tom.

"Giants are very big," Tom says. "So he will have big trousers and a big jacket."

Tom cuts out a green bit and makes the giant's trousers. Kate takes a blue bit and cuts it out to make his jacket.

"I'll cut out a black hat for the giant," says Kate.

"Now, we must make him look fierce," Tom tells Kate. "I'll cut this black bit out and put it here. That makes him look fierce."

"And I'll cut these blue bits out and put them here," Kate says. "Now he looks very fierce."

"These two bits can go there, then he is done," says Tom. They look at the giant.

"I don't like him much," says Kate. "He looks so very fierce."

''We have made the fierce giant. So now let's make a happy dwarf,'' Tom tells Kate.

They cut out some little yellow trousers and a little red jacket. Then they cut out a yellow hat for the dwarf.

''I'll cut out these little green bits and put them here,'' says Kate.

''He looks very happy,'' Tom tells her. Now they have to stick all the bits down onto the picture.

''I'll stick the giant's blue jacket here,'' Tom says. ''And you can put the green trousers there.''

Kate looks around for the green trousers. Where can they be? Where did she put them?

''The green trousers have gone,'' she tells Tom.

"I can't find them anywhere around here."

Then she looks at Sam.

"There they are," Kate says. "I've got the trousers now. I'll stick them here."

Sam looks at the picture they have done.

Then they find that they are walking up the green hill to the black castle. At first Sam is walking with them, then he goes running away up the hill to the castle. He runs right up to the red doors and goes inside. Kate looks at Tom.

"What do we do now?" she asks him.

"We will have to go and find Sam," Tom tells her.

"But I don't like this castle," she says. "It's too big and too black and too scary. The fierce giant will be inside, and he is too fierce."

"We've got to find Sam," Tom says. "We wouldn't let him stay in there would we?" So they walk on up the hill to the red doors of the castle.

Tom and Kate are not happy. They are talking about Sam. He has gone right inside the scary black castle. They wouldn't go home on their own, so they have to go and find him.

They go to the red doors. Kate tells Tom that the giant may be away, and that the dwarf may be on his own.

"The dwarf is happy. I would be very pleased to see him," she says. "But I don't want to see the giant at all."

"It will be a good thing if the dwarf is on his own," he tells her. "I don't like this scary castle much. But we shall have to go and find Sam."

So they look inside the castle.

"I can't see Sam anywhere inside there," Tom tells Kate.

"We will just have to go right in," he says. "But I don't like this at all."

They go right inside the castle and look around.

"Has he gone up there, do you think?" asks Kate.

"We will have to go and look," Tom tells her. They go all the way up but they don't see Sam anywhere.

"Where can he be?" Kate asks.

"He has got to be in this castle," Tom says.

They go down and look around. They can't see Sam at all.

"What's that?" asks Tom. "There is something over there."

"Look," Kate says. "It's just a black cat, running fast. It's like the one that I put in the picture and there are the kittens."

"Where shall we go now?" asks Kate. "Which door shall we open?"

They go to the yellow door and open it just a little way. When they look round the yellow door, they can see outside. The happy dwarf is on his own, giving the birds something to eat.

"He is just like we made him," Kate tells Tom. "He is very happy, giving the birds something to eat."

"Look over there," says Tom.
"That's the same cat and she has
two kittens with her."

They look at the cat with her kittens
running and jumping. Now the kittens
are going round and round.

"Well, that's not scary at all," says
Kate. "But Sam is not here."

"If Sam was here," Kate tells Tom, "he would be running after that black cat."

"I wouldn't let him," Tom says. "I just wouldn't let him go running after that cat and her kittens."

Which door will they open next? They look at all the doors around them.

"Let's open the pink one," Kate says.

So they go over to the pink door and open it just a little. They look round it. They can see the giant. He is very big and he looks very fierce. They can see him but he can't see them.

"Look, he's getting up. He's coming this way," says Tom. "No, he's walking over to the red box."

"Now he is looking in the red box," Kate tells him.

"He is taking something out. What is he getting?" asks Tom.

Kate and Tom are looking at the giant. The giant is sitting down and looking inside his red box and taking things out. He is taking out some of his treasure.

"Just look at all that," Tom tells Kate.

"Fantastic!" says Kate.

The giant takes out some big things and some little things. He likes all his treasure, but he looks very fierce. Kate and Tom don't want to talk to him at all.

"We have got to find Sam," Tom tells Kate. "Then we can go home."

But where can Sam be? They look at the doors.

"Which one shall we open this time?" asks Tom.

"It's taking us too long to find Sam," says Kate. "Where can he be?"

"Let's go to that door there, that orange one," Tom says. So they walk over to the orange door. It is open just a little, so that they can look round it.

"I can see the dwarf sitting over there," Kate tells Tom. "And there is Sam. He is sitting up and eating. Can you see him Tom, over there?"

"Now Sam is looking at us," Tom says. "But he's not coming over here. He wants to go on eating. And now the dwarf is giving him some more. We'll never get him away. He will never come now."

"The giant is coming in now," Kate tells Tom. "I don't like the look of him at all."

"What are we going to do?" asks Tom. "We can't just stay looking at them all day."

"The giant is sitting down," Kate tells Tom. "He may be good. He is giving Sam something to eat."

"You may be right," Tom says, "but I'm not going in there now."

They go on talking about the giant.

"Look now," Tom tells Kate. "The giant is getting up. And he's walking outside."

"The happy dwarf is talking to Sam,"
Kate says. "But I don't know what
he's saying."

The giant has gone now, so they can
go in.

"Come on, Kate, I'm going in," Tom
says. "We must
get Sam out."

The dwarf is
very pleased to
see them and
asks if they
would like
something to eat
and drink. They
tell him that they
have just come
to get Sam, and
they would like
to go before
the giant comes
back.

The dwarf asks them why they don't want to see the giant. Tom tells him that they think the giant is very scary.

Then the dwarf tells them about the giant. "He's not at all scary. He's a very good giant. But he will never be a happy giant. After all, you made him, so he will do everything that you want him to do."

"Sam must like him," says Kate, "or he would not be happy to stay here."

"Look," the dwarf tells them, "the giant is coming now. You can get to know him and you will see that he is not scary at all."

And the giant comes in.

The big fierce giant walks in and puts his jacket down. They don't like looking at him at all. Then Kate sees a big tear running down. She looks at the tear. Then she asks him why he is not happy.

The giant looks at Tom and Kate, and they see two more tears running down, then lots of tears.

"Why are you so sad?" Kate asks him.

"Well," says the giant, "just look at me. I look so fierce that no one likes me at all. You made me look fierce, but I am not fierce inside, I am happy inside. I'm very sad that I look so fierce. I have just one friend, and that is the dwarf. He knows why I am a sad giant."

"I know how we can help you," Tom tells the giant.

"As soon as we get home," Tom says, "we will make you into a happy giant."

"Yes," Kate tells him. "Then you will be happy for always and always."

The giant is surprised. He asks Tom and Kate to sit down and eat something. He gives them a drink of orange. Some cakes are blue and others are green. Kate takes a blue one and Tom is eating a green one.

They talk about the things that they like doing.

The giant is saying that he has made a boat, and he likes talking about it.

The dwarf says that he always likes to look at the birds and give them something to eat.

Kate and Tom say that they like to draw pictures and put in lots of things. Sam does not say anything.

"Before you go," says the giant, "come with me and see my treasure. We have to go to the pink door over there."

They go with the giant to the pink door. He opens his big red treasure box, and shows them all his treasure. Some bits are pink and yellow. Others are blue and green. But the bit of treasure that Kate likes best is orange.

"May I put it on, please?" she asks.

As she says this, she puts it on and looks at it.

The giant is getting out many things to show them. But Tom is very surprised.

"We did not draw this fantastic treasure in our picture," he tells the giant. "We did not think of it."

"No," says Kate. "But we did not draw anything inside the castle at all."

Tom says that it is time for them to go home. They thank the dwarf and the giant for all the things that they have had to eat.

The giant says that he is very pleased that they have been to the castle.

"So are we," Tom says, "and as soon as we get home, we'll make you into a happy giant."

"That will be a very good thing," the dwarf tells them.

"Come on, Sam, we have been here a long time," Kate says. "We have to go back. We are going home now."

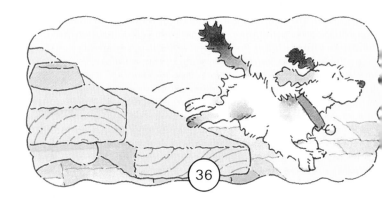

"Goodbye giant, goodbye dwarf," they say as they go off.

"Goodbye, come back and see us soon," say the giant and the dwarf. "We will always be happy to see you."

"We will come if we can," says Kate.

"But we don't know if we can," Tom tells her.

Tom and Kate are very busy now, doing their picture. Their mother tells them that it is time to eat. But Kate and Tom are saying that they have to do something first.

"I will take this off," says Kate, "and turn it round. If I stick it down this way round, the giant looks happy."

"And," Tom tells her, "if I stick these like this, he looks very happy."

"I like him much more now," says Kate.

"He will never be scary now," Tom tells her.

"What do you think, Sam?" she asks. "Is the giant happy now?

"He is saying 'Yes'," Kate tells Tom.

"How do you know that if he is not talking?" asks Tom.

"I just know," Kate says.

Their mother has been saying that it's time to eat.

"But, Mum," says Kate, "we have been to the castle and had lots to eat there. Now we are busy doing this."

"I had some green cakes," Tom says, "and Kate had some blue ones. And we had orange to drink."

"Well," says Mum, "I have no green or blue cakes, but I have got these pink ones. Have a pink cake?"

Then they tell their mum and dad all about the scary castle with two red doors. They tell them about the pink door with the treasure inside, and the yellow door with the dwarf and the birds, and the orange door with Sam eating.

"It's a fantastic picture," Dad tells them.

"Dad has put all the paper up," says Mum, "and I have been busy with the paint. So we have all had a good time."

Words introduced in this book

Number of words..................................50

LADYBIRD
READING SCHEMES

Ladybird reading schemes are suitable for use
with any other method of learning to read.

Say the Sounds

Ladybird's **Say the Sounds** graded reading scheme is a
phonics scheme. It teaches children the sounds of individual
letters and letter combinations, enabling them to tackle new
words by building them up as a blend of smaller units.

There are 8 titles in this scheme:

1 **Rocket to the jungle**
2 **Frog and the lollipops**
3 **The go-cart race**
4 **Pirate's treasure**

5 **Humpty Dumpty and the robots**
6 **Flying saucer**
7 **Dinosaur rescue**
8 **The accident**

Support material available: Practice Books, Double Cassette Pack,
Flash Cards